TO EVERYONE WHO WATERED THIS DREAM,

ESPECIALLY MY BIGGEST CHEERLEADER.

THIS IS FOR YOU.

VROOM!!

A speeding light and gust of wind knocked Barry over! When Barry got up, he couldn't believe his eyes.

What was that glowing under her feet??

She was moving faster than anything he saw! Barry always wanted to be fast like his friends. Barry asked, "What are those?"

SMACK!

Barry thought, "What if I can't?" He took another step and..

SMACK!!

At that moment, everyone laughed at Barry. Barry was embarrassed by the fall. He didn't feel big anymore . In fact he felt very small. At that moment, to him, ants were tall!

"You're too slow to race me!" Kari said as she took off.

Barry thought to himself, "What if they're right? What if I can never go fast?"

"Don't listen to them Barry! They have no idea what you can do!"

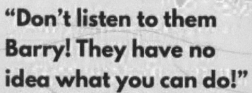

"Do you think she's right?" A soft voice said in the dust.

Barry answered nervously, "I don't know.. who's there?" He wasn't sure where he saw this face from, but as the dust began to clear, he realized who was there..

When Barry arrived the next morning, he couldn't believe his eyes. Tommy was moving faster than anything he ever saw. It was like he was everywhere at once! Barry was full of excitement! He had so many questions!

"You may not win THIS time, but you CAN control how hard you work and how you feel about it! Who knows, you may love it so much that you find yourself doing it all the time. Imagine how good you'll be then!" Tommy said.

"The more I practice the better I'll be!"
Barry realized.

"YES! Let's try our best and let the chips fall as they may." Tommy said.

"Chips? I thought we were skating!" Barry responded.

Tommy laughed, "We'll try our best and be proud of the results. We can get chips and dip after the race."

"LETS GO! " Barry roared.

SMACK!!

He tried to get up and he fell.

He tried

and he tried, and he tried

and he fell

and he fell

and he fell.

Kari took off! To her surprise though, Barry was right behind her. Barry was going fast!

With time running out, the Power Boost was Barry's only chance to win.

He thought to himself, "I think I can" He got low and boosted away..

This is what it must feel like to fly. He was higher than any bird in the sky.

He landed in a cloud of dust. Everyone was surprised at what they saw!